Threads

of

Unseen Fates

Sajid Azam

Love Story Of Annie and Jack

Annie grew up near a lake, a peaceful backdrop that contrasted with the stormy life she led. She was a generous girl by nature, but her heart carried the weight of her past. As a child, she lost both of her parents in a tragic car accident. Since then, she had been an orphan, living in an orphanage until she turned 18. Upon leaving, she took a job as a newspaper delivery girl, but the money barely covered her living expenses. To make things even harder, she was pursuing postgraduate studies, struggling to balance both work and school.

Annie had a tough exterior. She was a bit of a bully, covered in tattoos, with wild, colorful hair. She smoked cigarettes like a chimney, and she often went clubbing, hanging out with men she met there. The world had hardened her, and she shielded her vulnerability behind that tough persona.

Jack, on the other hand, was the opposite of Annie. A simple boy. He had recently moved to the city for his postgraduate studies and had a fascination with human behavior-he loved to understand how people reacted to the world around them. But when it came to dressing, he was hopeless, often wearing mismatched outfits that made him stand out in the worst way.

The First Meeting

Annie sat in class, absentmindedly staring at the board when a new boy entered the room. The teacher introduced him as Jack, and right away, his outfit stood out-a bizarre combination of bright colors that didn't match at all. The class snickered sofly, but Jack seemed unaware. The teacher pointed to the empty seat next to Annie, and Jack awkwardly made his way over, sitting beside her.

A few minutes into class, Jack realized he had forgotten his pen. He leaned toward Annie and asked, "Excuse me, can I borrow a pen?"

Annie, irritated, shot him a rude look but handed him a pen without a word. It was the first time they met, and it wasn't exactly a friendly start.

A Twist of Fate

Later that evening, Annie stood at the corner of a building, smoking a cigarette. She noticed a man running by, dressed in the same ridiculous outfit Jack had worn earlier. She thought nothing of it until, moments later, she saw Jack sprinting behind the man, desperately trying to catch up.

It was a funny sight-Jack and the thief were dressed in identical clothes, and the cops chasing after them couldn't tell who was who.

Jack caught sight of Annie and rushed over. "Please, help me!" he begged. "They think I'm the thief!"

Annie took a drag from her cigarette, amused by the situation. "Hide next to that dumpster," she said, tossing her jacket to him. "Put this on. I'll take care of it."

A few seconds later, two cops and a woman arrived, out of breath. "Did you see anyone wearing a yellow hoodie and brown pants?" one of the cops asked.

Annie, with a straight face, pointed to the right. "He went that way," she said, her tone so convincing that the cops immediately took off in that direction.

Once they were gone, she signaled to Jack that it was safe. Jack emerged from the shadows, covered in dirt and smelling terrible.

Annie wrinkled her nose but couldn't help feeling a little pity for him.

"Where do you live?" she asked.

Jack sheepishly gave her the location. "It's near to my place," she said.

"Alright, let's go," she said, waving down a cab. As they sat inside, Annie kept her hand over her nose, snickering all the way as the foul-smelling Jack sat beside her.

A Growing Connection

During the ride, Jack broke the silence. "Do you live with your parents?"

"No," Annie replied bluntly.

Jack, feeling the need to keep the conversation going. He said.

"I just moved here for postgrad," Jack explained. "I'm also looking for a part-time job."

They arrived at Annie's place, and as she stepped out of the cab, they heard a man shouting. It was Annie's landlord, yelling about overdue rent. Annie shouted back at him, unbothered by the scene.

Jack stood there, watching it all unfold.

The next day, in class, the teacher paired students for an assignment. To Jack's surprise-and Annie's dismay-they ended up as partners.

After class, Jack, curious about what he had witnessed the night before, asked Annie why the old man had been shouting at her.

Annie shrugged it off, but eventually said, "He was asking for rent. I'm out of money. Nobody buys newspapers anymore, and the company isn't paying me enough."

Jack thought for a moment, then said, "You could stay with me, at least until you get back on your feet."

Annie didn't respond at first, but later, after checking her account balance, she realized she was in trouble. She found Jack in the cafeteria and sat down. "Alright," she said, "show me your place."

A New Chapter

Annie followed Jack to his apartment. The moment she walked in, she was greeted by the sight of uncooked food, stacks of books, and a Playboy magazine hastily hidden under a pillow. Jack, clearly embarrassed, pretended like nothing was out of place, but Annie just smiled, amused by his awkwardness.

She decided to settle in. Jack found a job at a flower shop, and every morning Annie went to deliver newspapers. Their lives slowly began to sync, and despite their differences, they grew closer.

One day, on their way to university, they saw the thief again, still wearing the same outfit as Jack. The cops were once again in hot pursuit, and Annie couldn't stop laughing.

"Where on earth did you get those clothes?" she asked, wiping tears of laughter from her eyes.

Jack pointed to a nearby shop. "Buy one, get one free," he said sheepishly.

Annie shook her head but agreed to help Jack pick out better clothes. As they browsed the store, they spotted the same thief, once again buying outfits. It was too absurd for words.

Annie picked out some new clothes for Jack, and when he tried them on, he looked surprisingly good. She gave him an approving nod, and for the first time, she felt something shift inside her-a growing fondness for Jack.

A Carnival of Emotions

As they walked down the street, Jack spotted a carnival and excitedly suggested they go. Annie resisted at first, claiming she wasn't interested, but Jack managed to convince her.

At the carnival, they rode a rollercoaster. Annie, tough as she was, found herself screaming in fear, clutching Jack's hand and burying her head into his shoulder. Jack's heart swelled; his feelings for her were deepening.

They spent the rest of the day playing games. Annie surprised Jack by her shooting skills by hitting 10/10 perfect aim on a sharp shooting game and won him a small toy gun as a prize. It was a simple but meaningful gesture.

That night, they sat together in Jack's apartment. Annie, in a tank top, casually sat next to him on the sofa, teasing him about the TV show he was watching.

 Jack, unable to take his eyes off her, was mesmerized by her beauty.Jack was staring at her when Annie, without looking up, asked, "Why are you staring at me?"

Surprised, he replied, "I'm looking at your tattoos. They're impressive."

Jack's eyes caught the ink on Annie's arm. "That flower... it's beautiful."

Annie glanced at it. "It's a red spider lily."

"What does it mean?" Jack asked.

"It's the symbol of death," she said, her voice calm.

Jack hesitated. "Why that one?"

Annie's fingers grazed the tattoo. "Every tattoo has meaning. This one... reminds me that nothing lasts forever."

Jack held her gaze, sensing the depth behind her words but choosing not to ask more.

Annie looked at Jack with a smirk. "So, do you have a girlfriend?"

Jack shook his head, smiling. "Nah. I had one, but we broke up when she moved away, like two years ago."

He shot her a curious look. "What about you? Boyfriend?"

Annie grinned, her eyes gleaming with amusement. "Boyfriend? I've got a few," she said with a wink. " Sometimes it was a good experience, sometimes it was a bad experience."

She offered to take him to a club, promising to introduce him to some girls. Jack, unsure but intrigued, agreed.

The Club Incident

At the club, things took a turn.

The club was alive with music, lights flashing in sync with the beat as Annie and Jack downed one cocktail after another. The buzz of alcohol melted Jack's usual awkwardness, leaving him laughing louder, leaning closer, and relaxing in a way he usually didn't.

With a mischievous grin, Annie grabbed his arm, steering him toward a corner of the club where a striking dancer was performing under the lights. Jack's face went from amused to wide-eyed in a heartbeat, clearly unsure whether to watch or look away.

Annie leaned in, her voice dripping with teasing. "So, how about her? She does it for you?"

Jack turned bright red, shaking his head quickly. "Nah... not really," he mumbled, rubbing the back of his neck, pretending to be unimpressed.

"Seriously?" Annie laughed, folding her arms as she studied him, her eyes gleaming with playful challenge. "Alright then, let's go on a little mission. We'll find every girl in this club until you find one you like."

She tugged him through the crowd, pointing out girl after girl as Jack kept giving excuses, each one more ridiculous than the last.

Finally, Annie stopped, crossing her arms with a smirk. "You know, at this rate, I'll have to introduce you to everyone in the club before you find anyone even remotely interesting!"

Jack chuckled, cheeks flushed as he met her gaze. "Or maybe I'm just waiting for the right person to show up.

Though they decided to split and search for the perfect match, both Jack and Annie found themselves constantly searching for each other. Whenever Jack disappeared, Annie would feel uneasy, and Jack, in turn, would look for her whenever she wasn't in sight.

At one point, a girl approached Jack, distracting him. Meanwhile, Annie stepped outside for a cigarette.

But as she stood alone, a man from the club followed her and began to assault her.

Jack, realizing Annie was gone, frantically searched for her. When he finally found her, she was being choked by the man. Without thinking, Jack surged forward, but the man's punch struck him squarely, a thin line of blood appearing on Jack's face.

Annie, fueled by rage, pulled the man off Jack, but the attacker was relentless. Jack got back up and threw a strong right elbow, hitting the man square in the face. Annie grabbed a nearby hockey stick and struck the man in the knee, and together, they managed to fight him off.

They hurriedly left the club, catching a taxi just as the rain began to pour.

A Night of Passion

Back at home, Annie sat on Jack's lap, gently cleaning the blood from his nose. As she worked, Jack's hand moved to her tattoos, tracing the designs on her skin.He asked Annie about the meaning of her tattoos.

She said it's not a good time to discuss.His fingers found their way to a tattoo on her thigh, hidden beneath her dress. Annie didn't stop him, letting his touch linger.

Her breath quickened as Jack's hand moved upward, and in that moment, their desire for each other became undeniable. Annie allowed Jack to continue, her body responding to his touch. He pulled her close, and they kissed, the intensity of their emotions taking over.

They tumbled onto the bed, undressing each other in a frenzy. Their bodies moved together in a passionate, steamy night of love, each moment charged with the raw intensity of their attraction.

The next morning, Annie woke up first. She looked over at Jack, who was still asleep, and gave him a small kiss on the cheek before quietly heading out for her paper route. Jack, waking up late, smiled when he saw that Annie had left him breakfast.

A Shattered Dream

Jack woke up with a smile, savoring the memory of the night before. He ate the breakfast Annie had left for him, feeling a warm sense of contentment. That day at the flower shop, his routine was interrupted by a notification on his phone-an email regarding a job offer he'd applied for months ago. His heart skipped a beat. The company was offering him the position. Jack called Annie.

"I got the job," he said, a sigh of relief escaping him. He paused, glancing away before asking, "Would you... maybe want to go for dinner tonight?

"Annie smiled at the other end of the line, happy for him. "Alright, sounds good. See you tonight," she replied before hanging up.

That evening, Jack picked out a bouquet of flowers from the shop, one he had carefully arranged himself. As he crossed the street on his way to meet Annie, he didn't notice the speeding car coming his way. In a split second, the car slammed into him, sending the bouquet flying out of his hands. The world went dark.

A Heartbreak

Annie arrived at the restaurant first, waiting for Jack. Minutes turned into hours, and worry began to settle in. Just as she was about to call him, her phone rang.

The voice on the other end was cold and formal-it was from the hospital. Jack had been in an accident and was in critical condition.

Annie rushed to the hospital, her heart pounding in her chest.

When she arrived, they led her to the ICU. Through the glass, she saw Jack lying unconscious, hooked up to machines. His body was bruised, and he looked fragile-so different from the Jack she knew. A nurse handed her his clothes and personal belongings.

Among them was the earring she had lost during the fight at the club. Jack had held onto it, carefully.

Annie's breath caught in her throat as she realized just how much Jack cared for her. She entered the room, her legs trembling beneath her, and sat beside him.

Days turned into nights, and she barely left his side, waiting for him to wake up, praying for him to open his eyes.

Every day, Annie sat by Jack's bedside, her voice a constant companion in the silence of his coma. She shared the details of her life—small moments, fleeting thoughts—hoping that, somewhere deep inside, he could hear her. She wanted him to feel her presence, to know he wasn't alone, that there was still something worth waking up for. She refused to let him lose hope, willing him to fight, to come back to her.

Her friends called again, inviting her to a house party, their voices gentle but firm as they tried to pull her back to a life without Jack. 'You need to let go,' they urged, 'He might never wake up.' But Annie couldn't. Every time she closed her eyes, Jack was there—his smile, his awkward charm, the warmth of his presence. The past clung to her, wrapping her in memories too vivid to forget. How could they expect her to move on when her heart still beat for him? No, she wouldn't give up. Not while there was still the smallest glimmer of hope, even if no one else believed.

A Confession of Pain

One night, after weeks of waiting, Annie couldn't hold back the flood of emotions anymore. She took Jack's hand, even though he was still unconscious, and began to speak. Her voice was quiet, trembling with the weight of the memories she had buried for so long.

"You know, Jack, my real name isn't even Annie," she began, her voice shaky. "It's Aniston. I was born in the River Thames. I haven't told anyone this before, but I feel like I need to tell you."

She swallowed hard, her tears already starting to fall.

"I lost my parents when I was six. They died in a car crash, just like that," she said, her voice cracking. "After that, I lived with my aunt. But...her husband raped me. I remember screamed a lot but no one was there to help me .I was just a child, and my aunt knew. She didn't say anything because of her own kids. She sent me away to an orphanage to protect her family.

she murmured, her voice cracking. "Like something broken and thrown away...bruised, bloodied, and forgotten"

Annie wiped her tears, but more came flooding down.

"I spent my childhood alone, in that orphanage, every day wondering why no one cared about me.

Why did I have to suffer so much? I built walls around myself, tried to become tough so no one could ever hurt me again."

She squeezed Jack's hand tighter, her heart breaking open.

"But then I met you, Jack. You were different. You didn't see me as broken or damaged. You didn't judge me for who I had become. And for the first time, I felt like I could trust someone again. I felt safe with you."

Annie's voice dropped to a whisper, her tears now streaming freely.

"I love you, Jack. I've never said it before, but I do. I need you to wake up. Please...I can't lose you too."

"I waited for you at the restaurant, you know? Part of me wishes I'd just turned down that dinner request. We could've been at home, sharing some terrible, burnt food together," she said with a soft smile, trying to lighten the moment. She paused, her eyes fixed on him. "But it's okay. You just focus on getting better. I'll be here every day. There's nothing to worry about. We have so many more dates waiting for us."

She leaned over, pressing a soft kiss to his forehead before leaving the room, unaware that Jack's fingers twitched ever so slightly as if trying to respond.

A Glimmer of Hope

3 months passed, but something was changing. Jack's condition was improving, though he remained in a coma. Annie spent every waking moment by his side, hoping for a miracle.

One day, while she was in the cafeteria, the hospital called her urgently back to the room.

When she arrived, her heart stopped. Jack's room was filled with doctors and nurses, all hovering over his bed. Confusion gripped her as she approached, but then she saw it -Jack's eyes were open. He was awake.

Annie's breath hitched. She rushed to his side, and without thinking, she yelled, "You fucking idiot!" before pulling off his oxygen mask and planting a fierce kiss on his lips.

The doctors laughed, celebrating with her. Annie didn't care about anything at that moment except that Jack was alive. Tears of relief flowed freely down her face as she grabbed his hand, holding it like she would never let go.

Rebuilding Life

A few weeks later, Jack was finally strong enough to be discharged. Annie helped him out of the hospital, supporting his weight as they stepped into the fresh air. The garden outside the hospital was in full bloom, and the world seemed alive again, vibrant with color.

As they walked slowly, hand in hand, Annie looked up at Jack, her heart full. He looked back at her, his eyes filled with the same depth of emotion.

"I'm not going anywhere," Jack said softly.

END

If you enjoyed reading this book, please write at
azamsajid2929@gmail.com on Gmail. I would love to
hear from you!

About the Author

Sajid Azam, a native of Siwan, Bihar, is a data analyst by profession and a storyteller at heart. Inspired by the magic of Indian films, Sajid began writing to capture the intensity and nuances of human relationships. With his debut work, Threads of Unseen Fates, he delves into a world where love and resilience intertwine, creating a story that resonates deeply with readers.

Combining analytical skills with a profound interest in human emotions, Sajid crafts narratives that are both logical and deeply heartfelt. For him, writing is a journey—one he hopes to continue, bringing more unforgettable characters and moments to his readers.